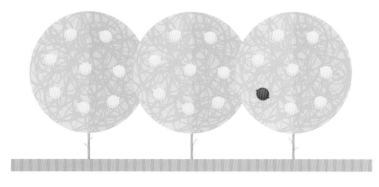

The Red Lemon

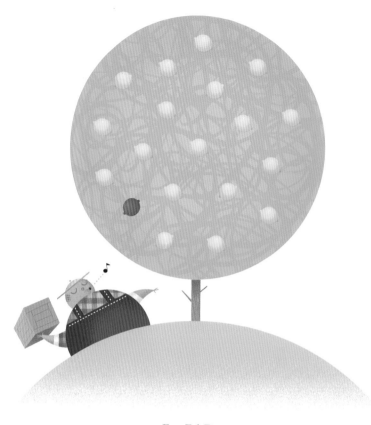

For Ed Dyson

Copyright © 2006 by Bob Staake. All rights reserved. Published in the United States by Golden Books, an imprint of Random House Children's Books, a division of Random House, Inc., New York. GOLDEN BOOKS, A GOLDEN BOOK, A LITTLE GOLDEN BOOK, and the G colophon are registered trademarks of Random House, Inc.
www.goldenbooks.com
www.randomhouse.com/kids
Educators and librarians, for a variety of teaching tools, visit us at
www.randomhouse.com/teachers
Library of Congress Cataloging-in-Publication Data
Staake, Bob.
The red lemon / by Bob Staake.—1st ed.
p. cm.
SUMMARY: Farmer McPhee's yellow lemons are ready to be picked and made into lemonade, pies, and muffins, but when a red lemon is found in the crop and discarded, it eventually yields some surprises.
ISBN 0-375-83593-8 (trade) — ISBN 0-375-93593-2 (lib. bdg.)
ISBN-13 978-0-375-83593-3 (trade) — ISBN-13 978-0-375-93593-0 (lib. bdg.)
[1. Lemon—Fiction. 2. Stories in rhyme.] I. Title.
PZ8.3.S778Red 2006   [E]—dc22   2005009854
PRINTED IN MALAYSIA   First Edition 2006
10 9 8 7 6 5 4 3

The Red Lemon

by Bob Staake

A Golden Book • New York

O ver the hills
and along the blue sea,

"The lemons are ready!" shouts Farmer McPhee.

"They soaked up the sun,
and drank all the rain.
We'll pick 'em and ship 'em
to stores via train!

"There's nothing like lemons.
This fruit isn't mellow.

They're tangy!
They're tasty!
They're tart—
and soooooo
yellow!"

Bright yellow lemons for miles and miles!
Bright yellow lemons give farmers big smiles!

Lemons
for sherbet and
lemons for pie!

Lemons
for drinks on
the Fourth of July!

Lemons
for cookies and
sweet birthday cakes!

Lemons
for muffins and
fresh fruity shakes!

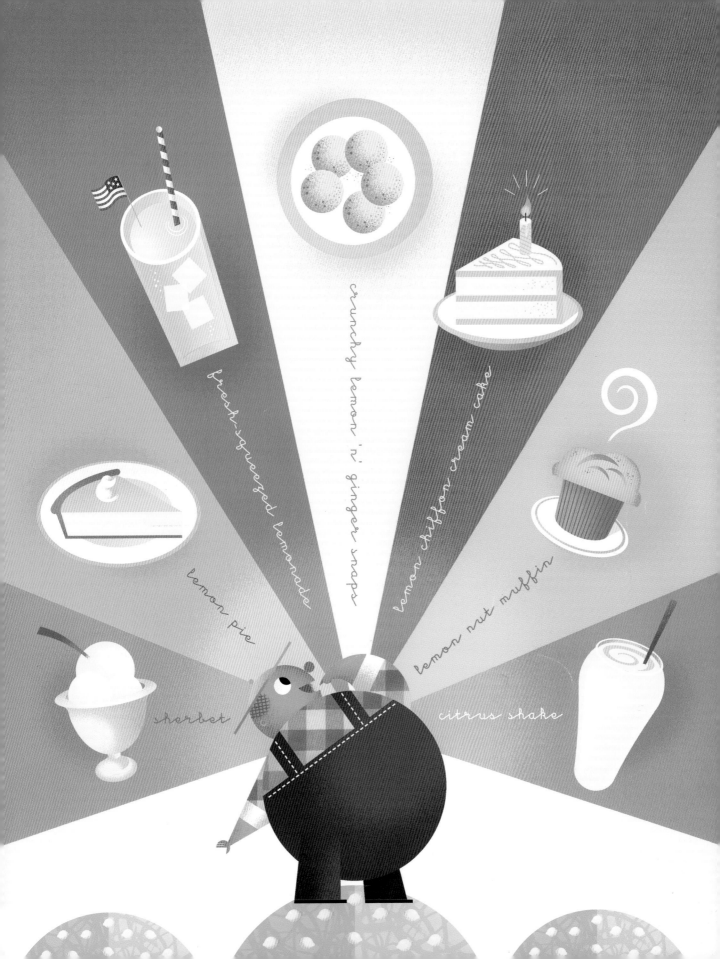

SNIFF 'em, and **PICK** 'em, and **PACK** 'em in a crate.

Bright yellow lemons, so tasty, so great!

"Wait just a minute!
That one overhead!
That lemon's not yellow.
My goodness, it's *red!*

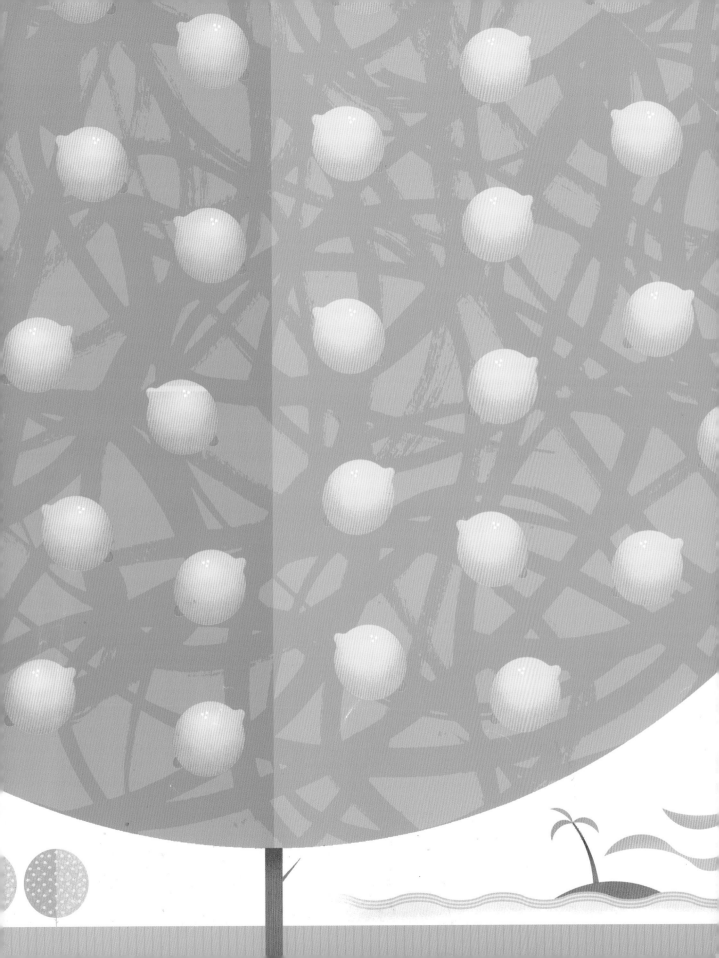

"It's as red as a stop sign!
It's as red as a rose!
I can't have red lemons
where yellow fruit grows!
Imagine a world where
lemonade's red!
Where once-yellow cupcakes
are crimson instead!

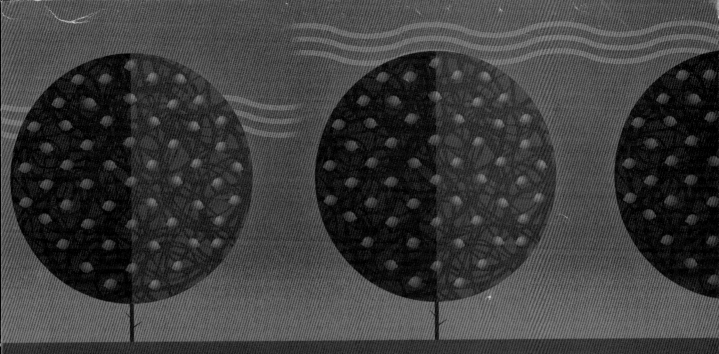

"When people bite into a
fruit that they chew,
they count on it being
the *right*-colored hue!
Who'd squeeze this *red* thing
in their afternoon tea?
Who'd buy a *red* lemon
from Farmer McPhee?

"This lemon
must go!
It's too red
to bear!
And so this
red lemon
I'll . . .

. . . toss over there!"

Then
many years passed
(two hundred, indeed).

That big lemon
orchard's now
nothing but
← -weed.

Yet on that small island,
up sprouted a seed.

It started as one
and soon became many—

Hotel Lemony

Peel's MARKET

LEMON scones $3

LEMON

OPEN 24 HOURS

ZEST old world cafe

RED NECTAR JUICEWORKS

YUMMY

FLY AIR RED

NEW FIRST CLASS Citruscruisers

LOFTS 733-5366

RED ECSTACY Lemonade

red lemon trees
in a grove of near twenty!

The islanders loved them,
those lemons of red.
They'd eat them in cupcakes
and bake them in bread.

And if yellow lemons
were always a treat,
the red lemon versions
were six times as sweet!

So now people travel
'cross oceans and seas
to eat the sweet fruit . . .

. . . from the red lemon trees.